Big Trouble for

Nellie Choc-Ice

JEREMY STRONG

Big Trouble for

Nellie
Choc-Ice

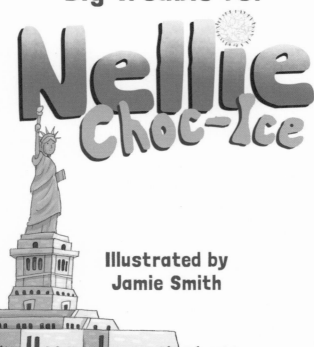

Illustrated by
Jamie Smith

Barrington Stoke

First published in 2018 in Great Britain by
Barrington Stoke Ltd
18 Walker Street, Edinburgh, EH3 7LP

www.barringtonstoke.co.uk

Text © 2018 Jeremy Strong
Illustrations © 2018 Jamie Smith

A CIP catalogue record for this book is available
from the British Library upon request

ISBN: 978-1-78112-766-7

Printed in China by Leo

This book is in a super readable format for young readers
beginning their independent reading journey.

*This is for penguins of all kinds – big
and little, fat and thin, black, white and all
shades between, but especially for penguins
with problems, and for helpful beardy
(and non-beardy) captains.*

Contents

Chapter 1
Mistakes

Nellie Choc-Ice is a penguin – a
Macaroni Penguin to be exact. If you
don't think there's any such thing as a
Macaroni Penguin, you would be wrong.
You can check it for yourself. If you
look up 'Macaroni Penguin' online, you
will see lots of lovely pictures.

But this is not why Nellie Choc-Ice is interesting or famous. You see, Nellie is VERY interesting and really quite famous too. "Why is that?" I hear you ask. You did ask, didn't you? So let me tell you.

Nellie Choc-Ice is the greatest penguin-explorer the world has ever known. In fact, she was the first

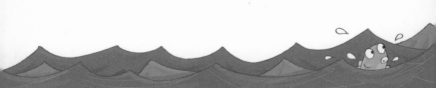

penguin EVER to travel from the South Pole, where she lived, all the way up to the North Pole, where she didn't live. But that is a story in another book.

Nellie didn't go on this journey on purpose. It was a MISTAKE – a big one, which is why I have put it in big letters. Nellie Choc-Ice often makes MISTAKES, as you are about to find out for yourself.

When Nellie found that she had arrived at the North Pole by MISTAKE, she knew she needed to go home, back to the South Pole. Luckily a nice submarine came along, a bit like a bus but underwater. It stopped at the North Pole and Captain Beardy-Beard spotted Nellie with his periscope.

"I'll take you back home to the South Pole," he told her. That was helpful of him, wasn't it?

It made Nellie very happy. You see, Nellie has got lots and lots of friends and family at the South Pole, as well as Small-Ma and Small-Pa. And she was missing them a lot.

So she climbed on to Captain Beardy-Beard's submarine and scrambled down the hatch.

BUT Nellie left the hatch door open. That was MISTAKE Number Two. If the submarine went underwater with the hatch open, then all the water in the sea would come flooding in. It was lucky that Jez spotted the open door. Jez was a member of the submarine crew.

He shut the hatch door.

Clang! Bang! And off they went. Brrrrm brrrrm brrrrm.

Nellie was very surprised that the submarine could stay underwater for such a long time.

"How does it breathe?" she asked Captain Beardy-Beard.

He laughed and said that the submarine didn't need to breathe. "It's a machine," he told her.

Nellie didn't know what a machine was but she nodded all the same. You see, she didn't want to feel stupid, so she pretended to know. Maybe you've done that too, sometimes? Nobody likes to feel that they don't know something.

They sailed on and on in the submarine. There wasn't much to see under the water, but Nellie enjoyed looking out of the little round windows. She liked to spot fish. She was very good at spotting fish. Most penguins are and that is because they like to eat fish. Pretty soon Nellie began to feel hungry.

BUT there was a problem with the submarine.

"Something is wrong with the engine, Captain," Jez said. "It's making a funny noise."

Oh dear!

Chapter 2

What Is That Funny Noise?

Everyone in the crew stopped work and listened to the funny noise in the submarine. Yes, there it was again – an odd rumbly-grumbly sound.

The crew went to the engine room, but that wasn't where the noise was coming from. That was a big surprise. If it wasn't the engine, what on earth was it?

"I'll help you," Nellie told Captain Beardy-Beard. She thought that if she helped, it would take her mind off how hungry she was. And so she followed the Captain.

He shook his head. "It's very odd," he said. "That noise is even louder now, but I still can't tell where it is coming from. It's almost as if the noise is following me."

"Yes. I can hear it too," Nellie Choc-Ice said. "It's very loud, isn't it?"

Captain Beardy-Beard looked at the little penguin. He put his hands on his hips and frowned.

"Nellie Choc-Ice! I do declare that rumbly-grumbly noise is coming from YOU!"

"Me?" Nellie cried.

"Yes, you! I think you must be hungry. It's your rumbly-grumbly tummy that is making all that noise. Your tummy sounds like an earthquake!"

"I think you mean a tummy-quake, Captain," Jez said with a smile and a wink at Nellie.

"Well, I am a little bit hungry, as it happens," Nellie agreed. "I've been watching the mackerel swim about in the sea and I do like mackerel. Maybe we can stop and have some tea?"

So they did. And it was a very nice tea, with sponge cake for the crew and fishcake for Nellie. After tea, Nellie said "thank you" to the Captain because even if she sometimes made MISTAKES she was also a very polite penguin and had very good manners.

The crew caught lots more mackerel for Nellie. They put it in the freezer so that there would always be some mackerel for Nellie even when the submarine was deep under the sea. You wouldn't want to run out of food, would you? Of course not. You might have a tummy-quake.

*

The submarine sailed on for another three days. On the fourth day, Jez checked all the controls and buttons on the submarine and went to Captain Beardy-Beard.

"Sorry to report, Captain," he said with a smart salute. "We seem to be low on diesel."

Nellie Choc-Ice heard Jez talking to the Captain. She asked them what "diesel" was.

Captain Beardy-Beard tried to explain. "We need diesel! It's what makes the submarine go."

"How does diesel work?" Nellie asked. She always had more questions than answers.

Jez smiled. "Well," he began. "Diesel is fuel. It's a sort of energy. Like when you eat mackerel and the mackerel gives you energy and helps you go."

Nellie jumped up and down. "I love to eat mackerel!" she said.

Jez nodded. "Well, the submarine eats diesel for its fuel and that is what makes the submarine go."

Nellie nodded and this time she really did understand. She didn't feel stupid at all.

Captain Beardy-Beard patted Nellie's head. "Don't worry," he told her. "We are close to New York. We shall put into port there and pick up some diesel."

And that is what they did.

When they got to New York, Captain Beardy-Beard and most of the crew went off to get the diesel.

Nellie was left on board the submarine with two members of the crew to look after her.

That was because the Captain didn't want Nellie to wander off and get lost in the big city.

But getting lost was not the problem at all. No, something far more dangerous was about to happen.

Oh dear!

Chapter 3

Something Far More Dangerous

Nellie sat in Jez's cabin and stared out of the window. She was getting VERY bored. New York looked so exciting. The buildings were HUGE!

"Are the buildings so tall because they need to hold up the sky?" Nellie asked herself. "Maybe the sky over New York is very wobbly."

All of a sudden there was a loud bang bang BANG – and Nellie had to stop thinking about New York!

Then there was a lot of shouting and running about. After that, there was a noisy splash. And after that, another noisy splash.

Nellie thought she heard a gurgly shout of "HELP!" But it might have been "HELF!" Nellie knew that "helf" wasn't even a real word, so she took no notice. That was a MISTAKE.

All of a sudden the door to Jez's cabin was almost smashed off its frame and a big man burst into the room. Nellie took one look at the man and she started to giggle.

The man was wearing a paper bag on his head with two eye-holes cut into it so he could see.

"DON'T YOU LAUGH AT ME!" the man yelled, and he pointed a toy Space-Gun at Nellie. "This is a hijack!"

Nellie had no idea what a hijack was. She thought it must be a way of saying "hello" – like "Hi Sam!" or "Hi Joe!"

"Hi Jack," she said with a giggle.

"That's right," the big man growled. "Now, take me to Panama."

Nellie scratched one foot with her other foot. "Sorry, Jack," she said. "I don't know anyone called Panama. Can you see all right with that bag on your head?"

"Of course I can, bird brain," the big man growled, "and my name isn't Jack."

"Oh, I thought you said it was. Why are you wearing a bag on your head?" Nellie asked.

"It's a mask, bird brain, so nobody will recognise me," the big man shouted.

"But it's so easy to recognise you," cried Nellie. "You've got a bag on your head!"

"Bird brain!" the man yelled. "Take me to Panama!"

Nellie was getting cross. The big man was so noisy and rude. He had no manners at all.

"I told you," she snapped. "I don't know who Panama is."

"It's a country, not a person, bird brain! Now take me there," the big man shouted. He waved his Space-Gun at her again.

"You don't have to shout," Nellie told him. "Why don't you ask nicely? Good manners don't cost anything. Small-Pa told me that and Small-Ma never shouted at me either, even when I bit her foot by mistake and it made her jump and she fell off her iceberg and—"

"SHUT UP AND TAKE ME TO PANAMA!" the big man yelled. "The cops are on my tail."

Nellie didn't understand that at all. Cops? Tail? The big man didn't have a tail. Nellie looked and looked at him but there was no tail. And if there was no tail, how could it have cops on it? And what were cops anyway?

Nellie was very puzzled but she went off to see what she could do to help.

Nellie liked to help. Maybe you like to help too. It's good to do something useful, isn't it?

Nellie pushed some buttons to get the engine to start, but nothing happened. Then she remembered what Jez had told the Captain – there was no diesel left. The submarine couldn't go anywhere without more diesel.

Nellie scratched one foot with the other again. She was thinking hard. Suddenly she had the answer. The submarine needed fuel – something to give it energy, and what gave Nellie energy was fish – and lots of it.

Was Nellie Choc-Ice going to make another MISTAKE?

Chapter 4

Nellie Makes Another Mistake

Nellie got some mackerel from the freezer and pushed it into the submarine's fuel tank. She pressed the button for the engine, but it still wouldn't start.

"Not enough food," Nellie muttered to herself. "This submarine must have a very, very big tummy." She began to push lots more mackerel into the tank.

"Why aren't we going?" the big man shouted. He was waving his plastic gun again and getting very hot and cross. "Come on, hurry up! I told you the cops are on my tail, bird brain!"

Nellie stopped what she was doing and folded her flippers across her chest.

"Now you just listen to me, Jack. I am not a bird brain," she said. "At least, I am a bird and I do have a brain, so in some ways I am a bird brain but not in the way you think. You can stop talking rubbish and going on about your tail, because you don't have one and in any case I don't care what cops are because you haven't got any of those either."

If Nellie thought her big speech was going to help her she was very wrong. It only made the big man much more angry and much more dangerous.

The big man's eyes went all angry and narrow. (Nellie could see this even though the big man had a paper bag over his head.) The big man stopped shouting and now he began to hiss like a snake, a very big and deadly snake.

He spoke slowly, in capital letters, like this –

"TSSSSSSSS! TAKE – ME – TO – PANAMA! TSSSSSSSSSSS!"

The big man pointed his gun at Nellie's head. Even Nellie knew she was in trouble. She didn't know the gun was just a toy. Her bird brain had to think of something very fast. She needed some more time. If she could keep the big man busy, then Captain Beardy-Beard might come back and save her.

"I've told you I don't know where Panama is, but if you show me which way to go, then I can try to get you there."

Nellie gave the big man a cheerful smile.

"And I can't see properly with that gun pointing at me," she added, helpful as ever.

"Get up on deck," the big man ordered Nellie.

(My goodness, he's very bossy, isn't he? I'm surprised Nellie hasn't flippered him on the nose, very hard. Maybe it's because he's pointing a Space-Gun at her.)

So Nellie climbed up the ladder. Climbing ladders is difficult for a penguin, but it's amazing what you can do when there's a big man pointing a Space-Gun at you.

The big man came up behind Nellie, up on to the deck. He looked all around and muttered to himself.

"Panama, Panama. I think it's sort of over there." The big man waved his Space-Gun at the sea.

Nellie Choc-Ice waddled a bit closer to him. "Where that big statue is? The one with a big ice cream?"

The big man scowled. "That's not an ice cream, bird brain!" he said. "That is the Statue of Liberty and she's holding a flame."

"Oh. All right. So, where did you say Panama is?" Nellie asked as she crept even closer to the big man.

"Past the Statue of Liberty, bird brain! Out that way!" The big man pointed out to sea again.

And because he was pointing the Space-Gun out to sea, he wasn't pointing it at Nellie.

OH GOOD!

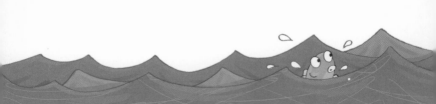

Chapter 5

Oh Good!

Hooray! The Space-Gun wasn't pointing at Nellie! She thought she might be able to take a stab at the big man's bottom.

So she did and it was a very big stab. Nellie stabbed as hard as she could with her very sharp beak.

Did it hurt the big man? YES! It hurt A LOT. Did he squeal? YES! He squealed like someone who had just had their bottom stabbed by a very cross penguin with a very sharp beak.

But had Nellie made a MISTAKE? No she had not.

"OWOWOWOWOWOWOWOWOW!"

The big man yelled, leaped up, slipped and fell overboard.

Splash!

And his Space-Gun fell overboard with him.

Another splash!

That was when two more things happened.

The first thing was Captain Beardy-Beard came back with Jez and the crew. The second thing was that Nellie saw two sailors splashing about in the water near the submarine. One of them kept shouting "HELF!" in a very gurgly voice. Of course he was really shouting "HELP!" but he had too much sea-water in his mouth to talk properly.

Now Nellie knew that the big man had thrown these two members of the crew overboard when he tried to hijack the submarine. She decided not to say anything this time, just in case she got into trouble for not helping them.

Of course Nellie didn't get into trouble. Everyone thought Nellie was a hero. It turned out that the big man was the most dangerous gangster in America. His name wasn't Jack, as you know. It was Mr Big.

A lot of people in uniform came to the submarine. Mr Big was very cross (and wet). He kept snarling at the people and calling them "stinking cops!" So then Nellie worked out that "cops" were in fact police officers. But she never did see Mr Big's tail. (I bet you know why!)

The police were very happy to catch Mr Big. They patted Nellie on the head and told her she was very brave and bold and wonderful and brilliant even if Mr Big only had a toy gun. (Nellie went a bit red when she heard that the Space-Gun was only a toy.) The Chief of Police said they should make a big statue of Nellie and stick it out in the sea right next to the Statue of Liberty.

"Can I have a big ice cream too?" Nellie asked.

The Chief of Police looked rather puzzled by that, but you know why Nellie asked, don't you?

Chapter 6
Oh Dear, Again

The next day the newspapers and TV news were full of the story of how Nellie Choc-Ice, the famous penguin-explorer, had caught Mr Big, America's most dangerous gangster. And so, for a while, everything was fine and wonderful.

But, at last, Captain Beardy-Beard
said that they really must get going and
carry on with their journey to the South
Pole.

"We are taking Nellie Choc-Ice back
home," he told reporters.

So the crew of the submarine got ready to leave America and set off for the South Pole. There was just one problem. It was a pretty BIG problem too.

The submarine's fuel tank was full of half-frozen mackerel.

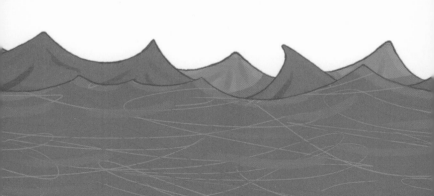

Was that a MISTAKE? Of course it was. It was a VERY BIG mistake indeed.

Oh dear, again.

*

And so Nellie's adventures were far from over. It's not easy to sort out problems like mackerel in the fuel tank, but that's another story.

Our books are tested
for children and young people by
children and young people.

Thanks to everyone who consulted on
a manuscript for their time and effort in
helping us to make our books better
for our readers.

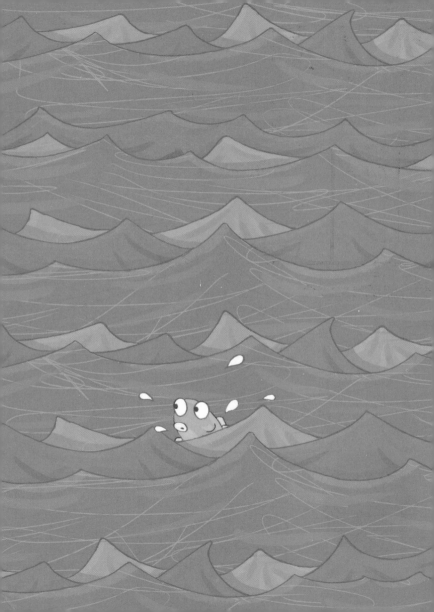